Power Trip

Jeffrey Nodelman

Illustrated by
Matthew C. Peters, Jeffrey Nodelman, Vinh Truong,
and Brian Donnelly

Power Trip is hand illustrated by the same
Grade A Quality Jumbo artists who bring you
Disney's Doug, the television series.

New York

SPECIAL EDITION

Original characters for "The Funnies" developed by Jim Jinkins and Joe Aaron.

Printed in the United States of America.

1 3 5 7 9 10 8 6 4 2

The artwork for this book is prepared using watercolor.

The text for this book is set in 18-point Century Schoolbook.

Library of Congress Catalog Card Number: 98-84122

ISBN:0-7868-4303-9

Power Trip

CHAPTER ONE

As Doug was taking his books out of his locker, he heard his name called over the loudspeaker. It was Vice Principal Bone, who said, "Doug Funnie, report to my office immediately." A chorus of "OOOHHHs" came from everyone standing in the halls.

Roger yelled out, "Hey, Funnie,

what did you do this time? Grand larceny? Burglary?"

Doug shrugged. He didn't know.

Doug walked slowly down the hallway to Mr. Bone's office, trying to think of why he could be in trouble. He had only been in school for a few minutes. Even Roger couldn't get in trouble that fast.

When Doug finally reached Mr. Bone's office, he still had no idea what he had done. He walked past a few students sitting nervously in the lobby and knocked on the door.

"Come in," Mr. Bone said. "Have a seat, Mr. Funnie."

Doug kept wondering why he was there.

"So . . . " Mr. Bone said. "Do you know why you're here?"

"No?" Doug gulped.

"Well, do you know what this is?" Mr. Bone asked, pointing to a fishbowl full of little crumpled-up pieces of paper.

"A fishbowl full of little crumpled-up pieces of paper," Doug replied.

"No, Mr. Funnie!" Mr. Bone stood. "It's your future! At exactly eight forty-five this morning, I pulled a name out of that fishbowl of the person to become the newest member of the BEEBE

BLUFF MIDDLE SCHOOL HALL MONITOR PATROL SQUAD! This is an elite group of students, specially handpicked by yours truly to keep order and safety in our hallowed halls. And do you know whose name I chose?"

"Mine?" Doug guessed, sinking deeper into his chair.

"Congratulations!" Mr. Bone said, handing Doug a bright orange sash. "Now, get out there and yell at anyone breaking the rules!"

"But, Mr. Bone," Doug said. "Do I have to? I don't think I'm cut out to be a hall monitor."

"Don't be ridiculous, Funnie!"

Mr. Bone snapped. “To be a member of the BEEBE BLUFF HALL MONITOR PATROL SQUAD is a great honor, and there’s no room for wishy-washy non–Patrol Squad types in their ranks. Your name was picked. It might have been by chance, but that's the chance we all have to take. Now, get out there and don't mess up!"

Doug left Mr. Bone's office thinking, why me?

CHAPTER TWO

As Doug was walking back to class, he noticed that everybody else was walking in the other direction. He saw Skeeter. "What's going on?"

"Principal White called an assembly in the auditorium," Skeeter answered. "And what's with the orange belt?"

"I'll tell you later," Doug said, shaking his head as they went off with the rest of their class.

As they took their seats, Principal White came onstage. "Good morning, Young Persons. I hope everyone is having a very special school year."

"Yeah." Doug frowned, looking down at his sash. "Great."

"By the way, this is an election year," Principal White continued. "So make sure that your parents are all registered to vote . . . for me. Anyway, the reason that I've called you here today is to introduce you to Police Officer Zac

Campbell of the Bluffington Police Department. He's here to talk to us about safety, so please listen up."

"This should be lame," Roger whispered to Willy as everyone else applauded.

Doug thought that being a cop was a lot like being a superhero, just without the X-ray vision. After all, isn't that what cops did, catch bad guys?

As if Officer Campbell read Doug's thoughts, he explained, "It's more than just catching bad guys. There is a lot of responsibility that goes along with wearing this badge. We protect people from those who break the law, kind of like the hall monitors here in your school. We both make it safe for you to go about your day."

Wow! Doug thought. Being a hall monitor is a lot like being a cop. He imagined the school hallway turning into a six-lane superhighway, and he was Doug Funnie . . . MOTORCYCLE COP! He sat at the side of the road, behind a billboard, radar gun at the ready. He watched as traffic went by, and then he saw a car in trouble! It was stranded in the middle lane. The car had smoke pouring out of the engine, and oil was leaking out the back! The driver was trapped, with no way to escape because of all the other cars zooming by. But wait! Officer Funnie knew the driver; it was Citizen Patti Mayonnaise! He quickly kick-started his motorcycle, and with lights flashing and siren blaring he sped off into the oncoming traffic. Doug rode effortlessly in and out of the other cars, but just as he was about to reach Patti, a huge truck cut him off. The only thing Doug could do was to pop a wheely and jump it! He floated in the air and landed perfectly next to Patti's car.

"Excuse me, but may I be of some

assistance, ma'am?" Officer Funnie asked, removing his helmet.

"Oh, thank you, Officer! You saved my life! How can I ever

thank you?" Patti said with her eyes gleaming up at his.

"Just doing my job, Miss. Hop on." In one smooth action, Officer Funnie pulled Patti onto the back of his motorcycle.

Patti swooned in delight. "Oh, Officer! You're so . . . police-y!" They rode off into the sunset together.

When Doug heard the applause, it took a minute for him to realize that it wasn't for him. The assembly was over. Everybody seemed really impressed with Officer Campbell.

Skeeter said, "My favorite part was when Officer Campbell showed us how to use his handcuffs on Roger. Honk, honk. What did you like, Doug?"

But before he had a chance to answer, Patti came over with Beebe and Connie.

"Hey, guys!" Patti said "Wasn't that policeman great?"

"And soooo cute!!" Beebe added.

"Did you see him smile as he

showed us how to direct traffic?"
Connie sighed. "Just dreamy."

Patti said, "It must be so gratifying to serve and protect. His mother must be very proud."

"Plus the cool uniform." Skeeter leaned forward to whisper to Doug. "Girls love the uniform!"

Doug looked at his orange hall monitor sash and thought, This might not be so bad. As he slipped it over his shoulder, Patti noticed and asked, "Is that a hall monitor's sash?"

"Yup." Doug smiled. "Vice Principal Bone handpicked me to join the squad today."

"That's so cool!" Patti exclaimed. "Now you're just like Officer Campbell."

Doug smiled and thought, if Patti's impressed, this might be worth it!

CHAPTER THREE

With five minutes left of the last class of the day, an announcement came over the loudspeaker: "ATTENTION . . . ALL HALL MONITORS TO THEIR POSTS."

Everybody looked up as Doug got up from his seat, put on his sash, and headed for the door. He overheard Connie say, "He's so lucky;

he gets to leave class early."

Doug headed out into the hallway, not as a civilian anymore, he thought, but as an officer of the law. But when he reached his post, he felt a little queasy. Doug was nervous. He realized that he had no idea what to do. So he just stood there, like a locker with a pulse.

The bell rang and all of the classrooms emptied out into the halls. Everyone walked past Doug, as if he weren't even there. Everybody but Roger.

As soon as he saw Doug he said, "Funnie, is that you?! You're the new hall monitor? HAH! This is

my road, you loser, and you're just a speed bump!"

Luckily, Mr. Bone came out of his office and interrupted Roger's taunts. "By the way, Mr. Funnie, I forgot to give you these this morning. Pink slips. Anyone who breaks the rules gets one of these invitations to detention," he said. "Speaking of detention, Mr. Klotz, don't you have somewhere to go?"

As they both walked away, Doug looked down at the pink slips. He felt a rush of power flow through him. It felt very cool.

CHAPTER FOUR

That night at dinner, Doug couldn't wait to tell his parents about his new job. They're going to be so proud of me, he thought. But every time he tried to talk about it, he was rudely interrupted.

First by his baby sister, Dirtbike. She was giving their

dad a workout by dropping her toys on the floor. By the time he bent down to pick one up, she had already dropped another one. This dance went on until Doug decided to help by double-teaming her.

At the next opportunity, Doug tried again to tell his news, but again was interrupted by an even bigger baby, his older sister, Judy. She rambled on and on about some audition she had for some play that no one had ever heard of. How important can playing a lamppost be, anyway? Doug wondered.

Finally, while they were cleaning up, Doug's mom asked him how his day was.

At last! Doug thought. But how to tell them? He said, "Oh the usual, I saw Patti, hung out with Skeeter, became a hall monitor."

"A hall monitor!" Doug's dad said,

picking up Dirtbike's toy. "Why, that's great, son! I can remember when I was in school—"

"Is it safe, dear?" Doug's mom interrupted.

"Of course it's safe," Doug said. "That's the whole point. I'm in charge of the safety for the entire hallway."

"HAH!" Judy laughed. "Doug,

you can't even be in charge of tying your own shoes!" she said, pointing at his open laces.

Even Dirtbike stopped torturing their dad long enough to give Doug a raspberry.

Later, he told his best nonhuman friend, Porkchop, "I'll show Judy! I'm gonna be the best hall monitor that this school has ever seen!"

"ROWF!" Porkchop agreed.

CHAPTER FIVE

On Tuesday morning, Doug took his post again. This time he stood in the middle of the hallway. He still didn't say anything, but anyone not moving in an orderly fashion got a stern look. As the thirty-second warning bell rang, everybody went into class. Everyone, that is, except Roger.

He walked right up to Doug.

“Hey, Funnie, I got a badge, too!” he said, pointing to a plastic toy badge inside his vest. “Funnie, you are such a loser—” BRRRINGGG! Roger got cut off by the bell.

This was the first time Doug had something to do besides stand around. Roger was late for class. But since this was Roger’s first strike, he would go easy on him. He said, “Roger, this time I’m only giving you a warning, but next time I can’t let you off so easy. Rules are rules.”

Roger’s jaw dropped. He was stunned, as was everyone in the

classroom watching through the open door. No one could believe that Doug had stood up to Roger like that, *especially* Roger!

"Funnie, I oughta pound you into the ground!" Roger threatened. But everyone was watching, so instead he slinked into class without his usual strut. As he sat down next to Willy, Boomer, and Ned, he swore he'd get back at Doug for humiliating him like that. He'd get Doug fired!

Out in the hall, Doug thought, That wasn't so bad. Maybe I *could* be good at this!

CHAPTER SIX

On Wednesday, Doug stood at his post. After his little run-in with Roger, he seemed much more confident. He had . . . ATTITUDE! Now he was much more vocal, too.

"Move along, people," Doug said. "Nothing to see here; just keep moving."

At that moment, Guy rushed in and said, "Doug, heard what happened yesterday with you and Roger. FABOO! Makes for a great story. You are a man on a mission, my friend, a man on a mission!" Guy never came to a complete stop. He rushed out as fast as he came in.

As Doug said, "Slow down, mister," he thought, man on a mission? Patti has got to be impressed! He imagined himself at the school assembly again, but now he wasn't sitting with his classmates. This time, he was up onstage. He was wearing a black suit, dark sunglasses, and he had

an earpiece sticking out of his left ear. He was standing next to Police Officer Campbell, who was holding a big, shiny medal.

Principal White said, "And the medal for the best hall monitor . . . EVER . . . goes to Beebe Bluff Middle School's very own Doug Funnie!"

Everybody cheered as Officer Campbell pinned the medal on Doug's chest.

Patti, sitting in the front row, yelled out, "Doug, you're the greatest!!!"

Doug smiled until he saw Roger walking by with his gang. Roger

was holding a clipboard and asking for signatures. He said, "Impeach Doug Funnie! He's no fun!" As the thirty-second warning bell rang, he looked over at Doug, who didn't say a word. He just pointed to the clock on the wall. Roger stomped away, mumbling to himself.

CHAPTER SEVEN

On Thursday, Doug stood on a stepladder in the middle of the hall. He was using a megaphone and barking orders. “Let’s go, people. Come on. This hallway is just a short trip to your next class, and if you don’t run, you won’t trip!”

Connie and Beebe were getting

books from their lockers when Doug noticed them and yelled out, “Hey, you guys, no dillydallying over there! Move along.”

Connie said, “He’s starting to give this school a bad name.”

“I know,” Beebe answered. “I gotta think about changing it!”

A second later, Patti ran by. She waved to Doug, who smiled at her as he said, “Hey, Patti, you’re gonna have to slow down! No running in the halls.”

Doug imagined himself as a drill sergeant. His job was to keep his troops in line, and if that meant he had to be tough, then that’s what he would do.

As Skeeter turned the corner and started to walk down Doug's hall, he noticed his friend was standing perfectly still. It didn't even look like he was blinking. Skeeter felt he had to do something, so he went over to Doug and said, “Hey, man. Honk, honk. How’s it going?”

Doug didn’t respond. He just stood there watching the hallway.

Skeeter tried again. “I said, hey, man. How’s it going?”

Still nothing.

Skeeter cupped his hands around his mouth and tried one

last time. "I said . . . HEY, MAN! HOW'S IT GOING?"

"Sorry, Skeet. I can't talk while I'm on duty," Doug said as he pulled a whistle out of his pocket and blew . . . TWEEET! "Hey, you over there! Slow down! Where's the fire?"

As Skeeter walked away, he asked himself, Where's my best friend?

That night at dinner, the first time Dirtbike dropped her spoon, before his dad had a chance to pick it up, Doug knelt down to get it. As he returned it to her, he shook his head and said, "No."

He told Judy, twice, to stop

talking with her mouth full. He even warned Porkchop that he came down the stairs too fast and didn't

use the handrail. As Porkchop looked at his paw, knowing he couldn't even reach the handrail, he rolled his eyes. It was pretty clear that this wasn't the Doug he knew. Doug was changing. His power was going to his head!

CHAPTER EIGHT

On Friday, Doug took his post again. He stood in the middle of the hallway, on top of the stepladder, holding his megaphone in one hand, twirling his whistle in his other hand. His eyes roamed the hallway like a hawk. If Patti could only see me now, he thought. He imagined that he would go down in history as Doug Funnie, the legendary hall monitor who finally brought peace to the treacherous hallways of Beebe Bluff Middle School.

Just then, moving through the crowd, rose a puff of dust and a barrage of flying papers. A hush came over the entire hallway as

they waited for Doug to pull over the latest offender. Doug knew who it was. It had to be Roger. This was it, he thought. No more Mr. Nice Guy! Running in the halls was a total violation of Mr. Bone's school rules, and if he didn't do something now, chaos would reign!

Doug steadied himself, reaching for a pink slip like a gunfighter in the old West. But as he pulled out the pad, he realized that he knew the speeder, and it wasn't Roger.

"Hey, Doug," Patti said in a hurry. "I can't talk right now. I'm late for gym class."

What could Doug do? He had already warned her once, and the whole school was watching.

Roger yelled out, "Get her, Funnie! She's a menace to civil-minded walkers everywhere!"

Doug dropped his head and said, "I'm sorry, Patti, but . . . but . . . ."

"But what, Doug?" Patti said. "I gotta go."

Doug tried not to make eye contact with her as he said, "No running in the halls," and handed the girl of his dreams a pink slip.

"What?!" Patti gasped! "You're

giving me detention? DETEN-
TION! Oh, Doug Funnie, you are such a . . . such a . . . HALL MONITOR!!!"

For the first time since Doug put on his sash, he began to see the consequences that went along with the power of his office, and he didn't like it one bit! He overheard Skeeter say, "He's worse than Vice Principal Bone!"

CHAPTER NINE

After school, Doug waited outside of detention hall for Patti to show up. How could this have happened? he asked himself. I was trying to impress Patti, and instead, I ended up giving her detention! He wanted to apologize. A lot. And maybe even beg forgiveness.

Unfortunately, Vice Principal Bone showed up first. He told Doug, "You're doing a bang-up job, Mr. Funnie. I didn't think you had it in you, but you remind me of myself when I was your age."

"Great," Doug sarcastically said to himself. "That makes me feel

much better." He took off his sash and handed it back to Vice Principal Bone.

"What's this?" Mr. Bone asked. "You're quitting?"

"No, not quitting. Retiring," Doug answered. "I guess I'm more of the follow-the-rules kind of guy than the enforce-the-rules kind of guy."

Patti overheard Doug as she walked up with Roger.

"Same seats as usual, Mr. Bone?" Roger asked as the two of them walked into the classroom.

"Hi, Patti," Doug said softly. "I'm sorry I gave you detention. I guess I got a little carried away."

"A little carried away?" Patti said. "You used a megaphone in a hallway that's only twenty feet long! We heard you all the way across the school in the girls' locker room while the basketball team was practicing!"

"Okay," Doug agreed. "A *lot* carried away. I'm sorry."

Patti admitted that it wasn't entirely his fault. After all, she *was* running in the halls, which *is* against the rules.

Trying to make peace, Doug asked, "When you're done in there, how about Swirly's?"

Patti said, "Sure, your treat."

"Deal!" Doug said, relieved.

As Patti turned to go into detention hall, she smiled back at Doug and said, "You know, you did look kind of cute in your little orange sash."

Doug smiled a little, embarrassed.

“Whoa, Doug, like the new duds, dude?” Skunky said as he walked toward Doug wearing a hall monitor’s sash. “Mr. Bone saw me over by my locker just now and handpicked me to be the newest member of the BEEBE BLUFF MIDDLE SCHOOL HALL MONITOR PATROL SQUAD . . .

Torquin', man!" He walked away yelling at a student running by. "Hey, man! Get a load of the orange sash, dude! This isn't like a race, you know."

WHOOPS!

Doug was about to take the attendance list to the school office. But he tripped in a trash can. Now all of the names are mixed up. He can't turn them over to Vice Principal Bone like that! Can you help Doug unscramble the names of all the kids in his class?

1. UDGO
2. TIATP
3. EGORR
4. KETRESE
5. YLAKHC
6. OMOBER
7. EDN
8. LYILW
9. NIENCO
10. NKUKSY
11. CKTUNREF
12. EBEEB

1. Doug **2.** Patti **3.** Roger **4.** Skeeter
5. Chalky **6.** Boomer **7.** Ned **8.** Willy
9. Connie **10.** Skunky **11.** Fentruck **12.** Beebe

A Brand Spanking New Book Series

CHECK THIS OUT!

Every Doug Chronicles book is jam-packed with special offers on cool Doug stuff. *Awesome!*

Available at your local bookstore
$3.95 each
Read them all!

Look for new Doug Chronicles every other month

Available Now
DOUG CHRONICLES #1
Lost in Space
ISBN 0-7868-4232-6

Available Now
DOUG CHRONICLES #2
Porkchop to the Rescue
ISBN 0-7868-4231-8

Available Now
DOUG CHRONICLES #3
A Picture for Patti
ISBN 0-7868-4236-9

Available Now
DOUG CHRONICLES #4
A Day with Dirtbike
ISBN 0-7868-4233-4

Available in August
DOUG CHRONICLES #5
Power Trip
ISBN 0-7868-4258-X

Available in October
DOUG CHRONICLES #6
Funnie Haunted House
ISBN 0-7868-4259-8

Available in December
DOUG CHRONICLES #7
Poor Roger
ISBN 0-7868-4260-1

Available February 1999
DOUG CHRONICLES #8
Winter Games
ISBN 0-7868-4264-4

Doug, Patti, Skeeter, Soft Friends From Mattel!